Harriet and George's
CHRISTMAS TREAT

Nancy ☆ Carlson

❦ Carolrhoda Books, Inc./ Minneapolis

Carolrhoda Books, Inc.
A division of Lerner Publishing Group
241 First Avenue North
Minneapolis, MN 55401 U.S.A.

Website address: www.lernerbooks.com

Library of Congress Cataloging-in-Publication Data

Carlson, Nancy L.
    Harriet and George's Christmas treat / by Nancy Carlson.
      p.   cm.
Summary: While getting ready for Christmas, Harriet and her
friend George try to avoid Ms. Hoozit and her fruitcake, only to
miss out on a yummy treat.
    ISBN 1-57505-506-6 (lib. bdg. : alk paper)
    [1. Fruitcake—Fiction. 2. Dogs—Fiction. 3. Rabbits—Fiction.
4. Christmas—Fiction.] I. Title.
PZ7.C21664 Haf 2001
[E]—dc21
                                                    00-010749

Manufactured in the United States of America
1 2 3 4 5 6 – JR – 06 05 04 03 02 01

To my friends at the Nutcracker Sweet, Barbie, Debbie, and Noni!

Thank you for all your wonderful work with children!!!

I still miss the mother's tea!

It was almost Christmas.

Harriet and George were going shopping when
they saw Ms. Hoozit leave the grocery store.

"Hi, Ms. Hoozit," said Harriet.

"Hi, kids," said Ms. Hoozit. "No time to talk.
I'm off to do my holiday baking. Now be sure to stop
over later for a Christmas treat!" Ms. Hoozit rushed away.

"Oh, no! Ms. Hoozit is going home to bake!"
said George.
"That can mean only one thing!" said Harriet.

"Ms. Hoozit is making fruitcake!"

"Remember last year when Ms. Hoozit made us try
a piece right in front of her?" said George.

"Yuck! It tasted awful," said Harriet.
"And I almost broke a tooth."

"Remember when you dropped Ms. Hoozit's
fruitcake on your foot?" said Harriet.
"Ouch! That really hurt!" said George.

"But it worked great for cracking nuts," he said.

"I'll never forget the time we used the fruitcake to play football," said Harriet.

"It almost hit your little brother," said George.
"That was a close call," said Harriet.
"Wow, fruitcake can be dangerous!"

"There is only one thing for us to do this Christmas," said Harriet.
"Avoid Ms. Hoozit and her fruitcake!" said George.

On Monday when Harriet and George
saw Ms. Hoozit shoveling,

On Tuesday when Harriet was helping
her dad put up Christmas lights,
Ms. Hoozit looked out her window.

they pulled down their hats
so she wouldn't recognize them.

So Harriet ducked behind a bush.

For the rest of the week,
Harriet and George hid from Ms. Hoozit.

By Friday, they were exhausted.
But it was worth it to avoid Ms. Hoozit's fruitcake.

On Christmas Eve, they saw Ms. Hoozit invite
Harriet's brother, Walt, in for a Christmas treat.

"Poor little pup," said George.
"Soon he'll be eating fruitcake," said Harriet.

When Walt finally came out of Ms. Hoozit's house
Harriet asked, "How was the fruitcake?"

"Ms. Hoozit made fudge this year?" said George.

Before Walt could answer, Ms. Hoozit opened the door.
"Well, there you two are," she said.
"Come in for a Christmas treat."
"OK!" said Harriet.
"Fudge!" whispered George.

"I made a big batch of fudge this year!"
said Ms. Hoozit.
"Oh, boy!" said Harriet.
"But I could never find you two . . .

". . . and my fudge is all gone. But don't worry,
I still have a Christmas treat for you."

"Last year's fruitcake!
Eat up and Merry Christmas!" said Ms. Hoozit.